《傲慢与偏见》
PRIDE AND PREJUDICE

艺术笔记

〔英〕简·奥斯丁 著
〔英〕休·汤姆森 绘
孙致礼 译

人民文学出版社

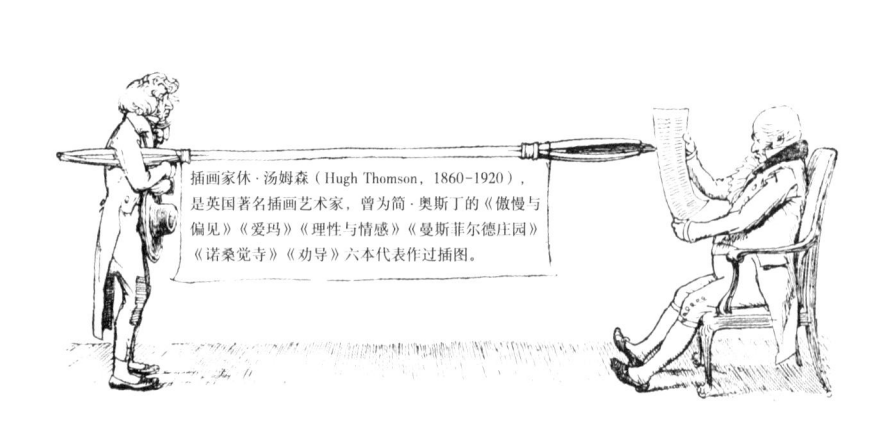

插画家休·汤姆森（Hugh Thomson，1860-1920），是英国著名插画艺术家，曾为简·奥斯丁的《傲慢与偏见》《爱玛》《理性与情感》《曼斯菲尔德庄园》《诺桑觉寺》《劝导》六本代表作过插图。

婚姻幸福完全是个机遇问题。
双方的脾气即使彼此非常熟悉，或者非常相似，
也不会给双方增添丝毫的幸福。
他们的脾气总是越来越不对劲，后来就引起了麻烦。
你既然要和一个人过一辈子，最好尽量少了解他的缺点。

Happiness in marriage is entirely a matter of chance.
If the dispositions of the parties are ever so well known to each other, or ever so similar before hand, it does not advance their felicity in the least.
They always continue to grow sufficiently unlike afterwards to have their share of vexation;
and it is better to know as little as possible of the defects of the person with whom you are to pass your life.

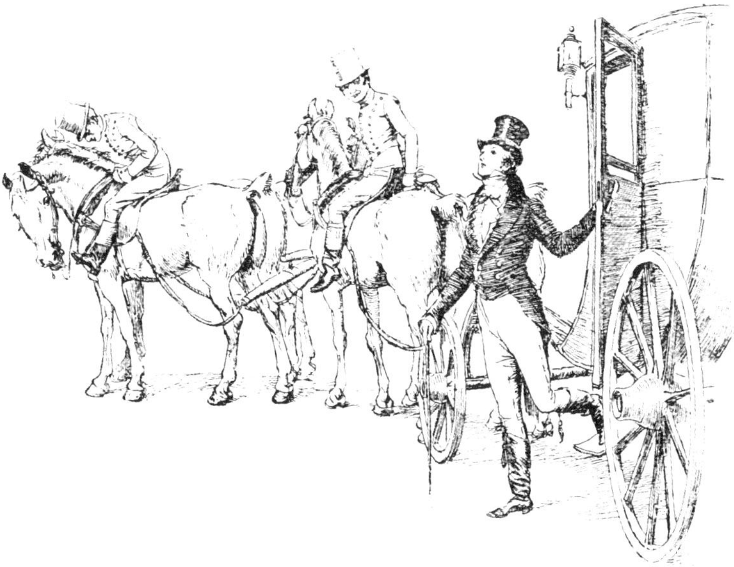

"We can all begin freely a slight preference is natural enough; but there are very few of us who have heart enough to be really in love without encouragement."

"男女恋爱大都含有感恩图报和爱慕虚荣的成分，因此听其自然是不保险的。开头可能都很随便——略有点好感本是很自然的事情，但是很少有人能在没有受到对方鼓励的情况下，敢于倾心相爱。"

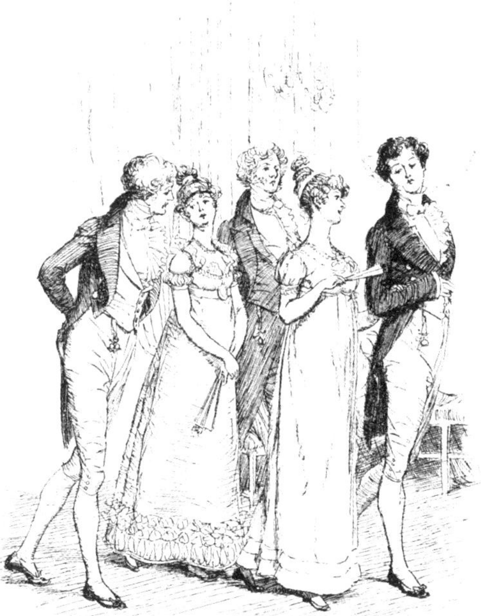

"假使他没有伤害我的自尊,我会很容易原谅他的骄傲。"
"I could easily forgive his pride, if he had not mortified mine."

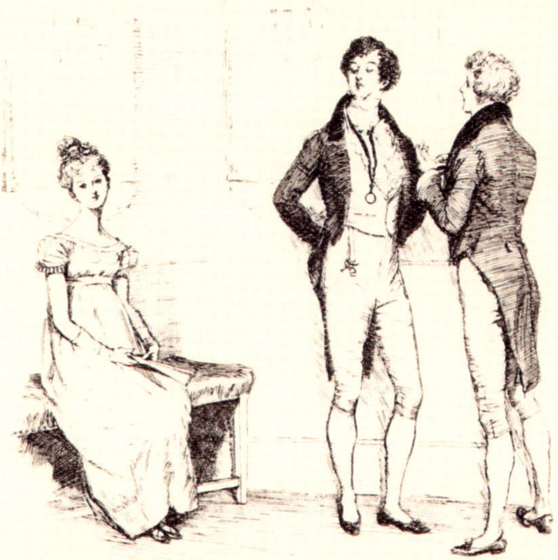

"Vanity and pride are different things, though the words are often used synonymously. A person may be proud without being vain. Pride relates more to our opinion of ourselves; vanity to what we would have others think of us."

"虚荣与骄傲是两个不同的概念,虽然两个字眼经常给当作同义词混用。一个人可以骄傲而不虚荣。骄傲多指我们对自己的看法,虚荣多指我们想要别人对我们抱有什么看法。"

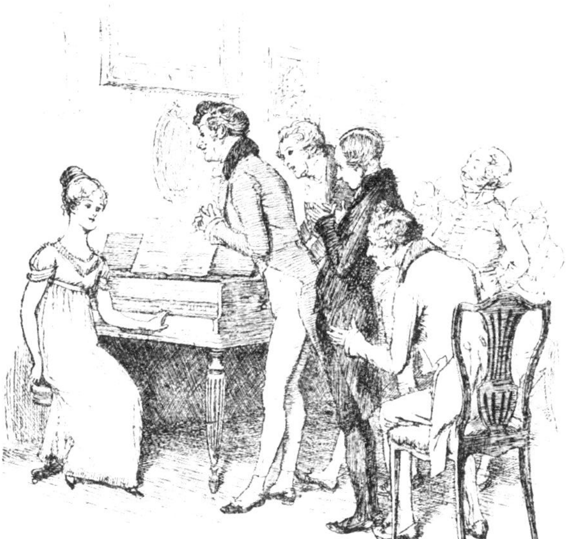

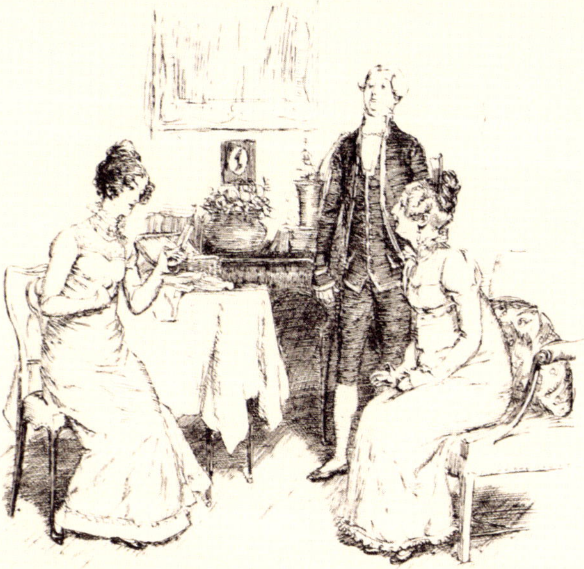

"不用啦,不用啦;你们就在这儿走走吧。"
"No, no; stay where you are."

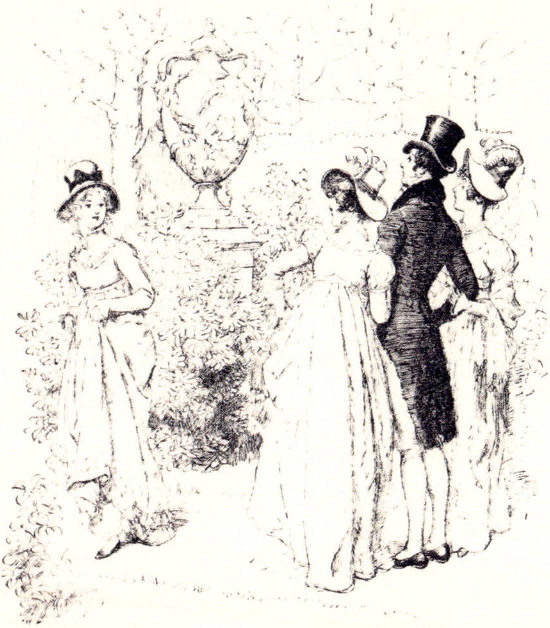

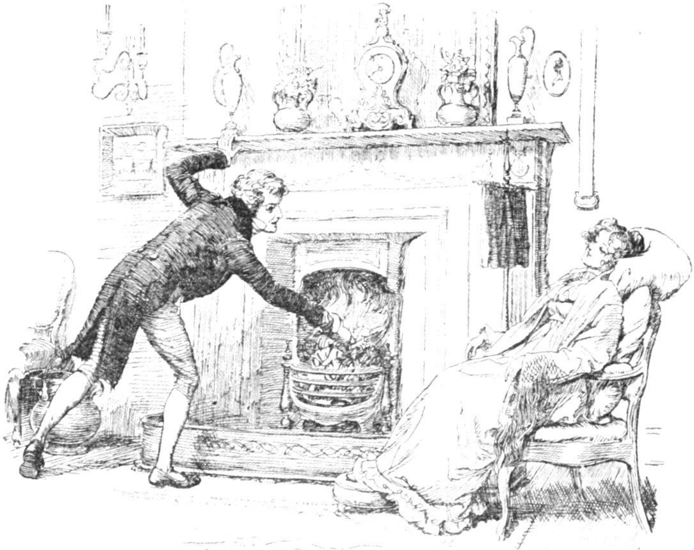

"...it was the only honourable provision for well-educated young women of small fortune, and, however uncertain of giving happiness, must be their pleasantest preservative from want."

"对于受过良好教育却没有多少财产的青年女子来说,嫁人是唯一的一条体面出路;尽管出嫁不一定会叫人幸福,但总归是女人最适意的保险箱,能确保她们不致挨冻受饥。"

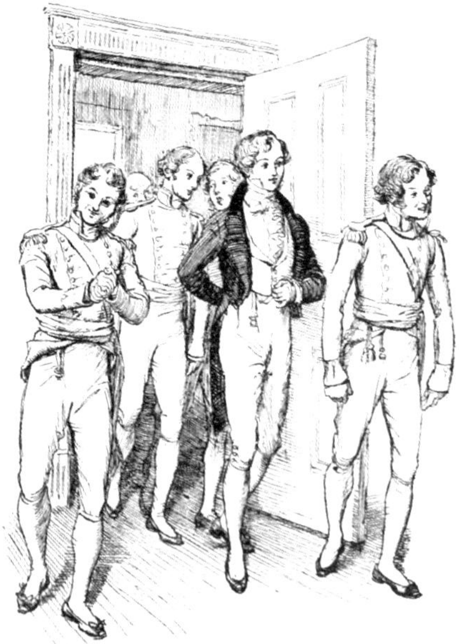

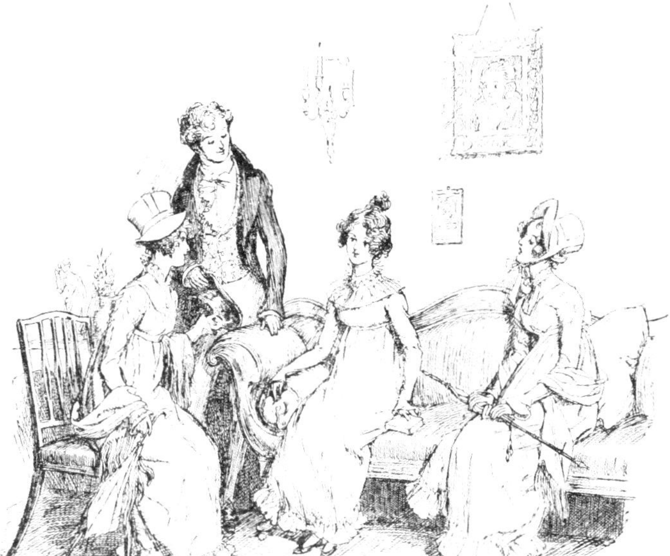

"...such very superior dancing is not often seen."
"舞跳得这么棒,真是少见。"

"...to assure you in the most animated language of the violence of my affection."

"只想用最激动的语言,向你倾诉一下我最炽烈的感情。"

"...for I have often observed, that resignation is never so perfect as when the blessing denied begins to lose somewhat of its value in our estimation."

"为我时常发现,幸福一经拒绝,在我们眼里也就不再显得那么珍贵。"

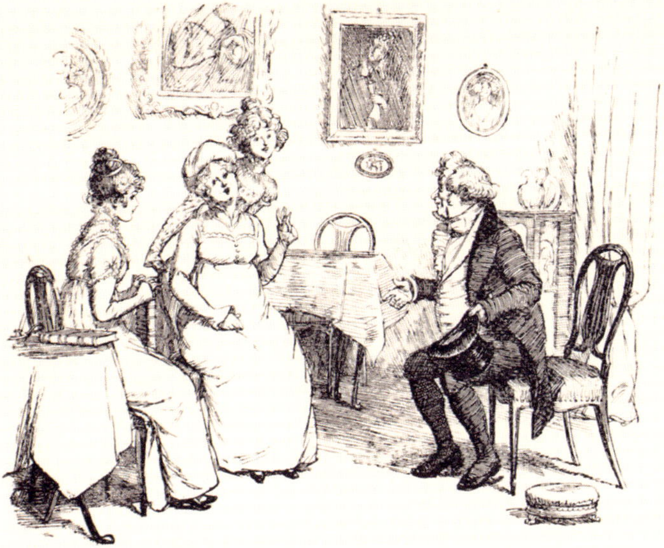

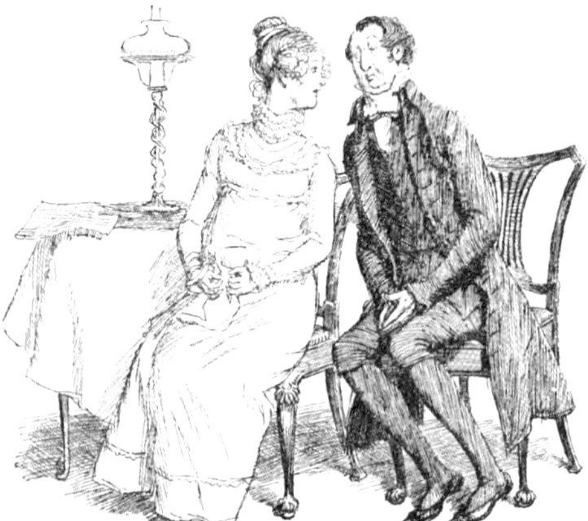

"handsome young men must have something to live on as well as the plain."

"美貌青年与相貌平常的人一样,也得有饭吃、有衣穿。"

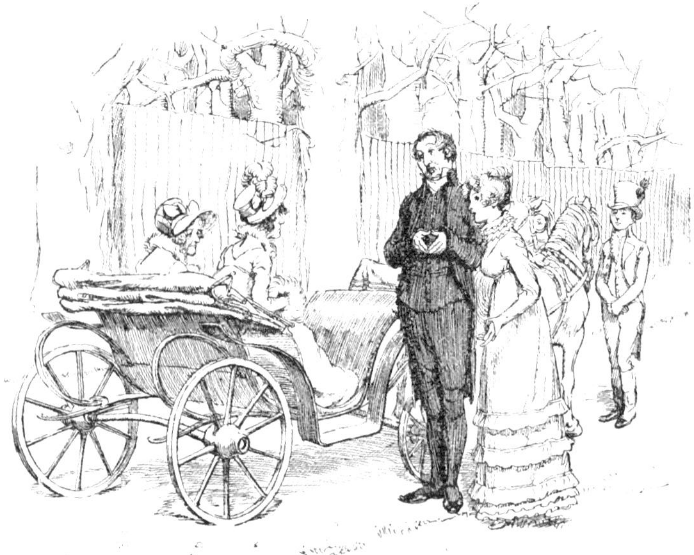

"咖苔琳夫人,你给了我一件珍宝。"

"...'Lady Catherine,' said she, 'you have given me a treasure.'..."

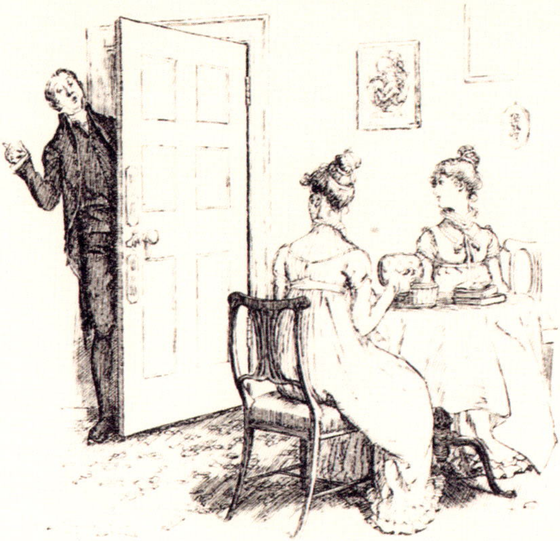

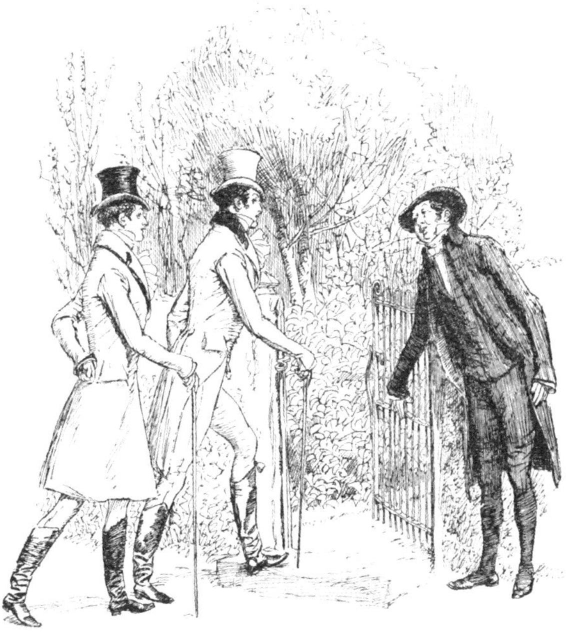

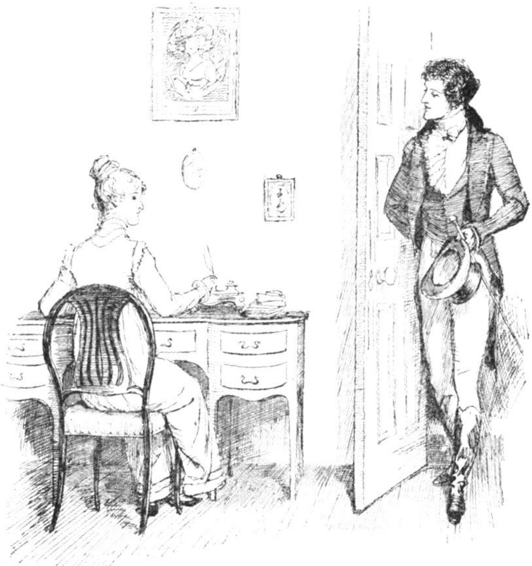

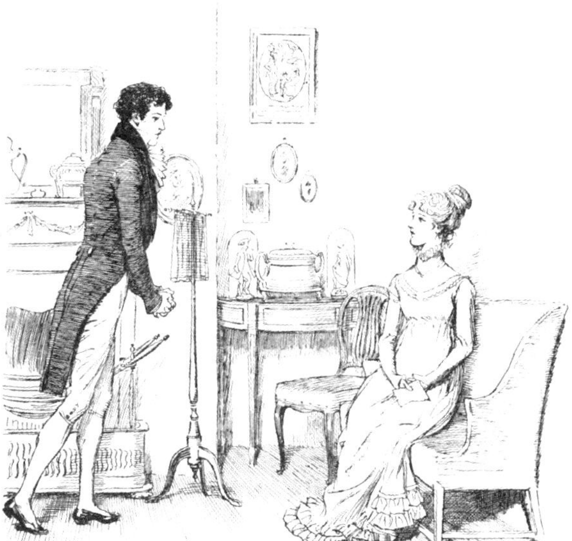

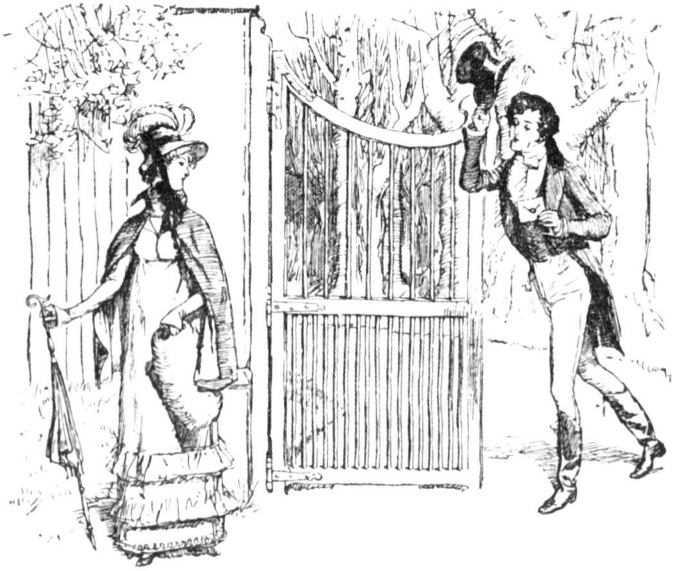

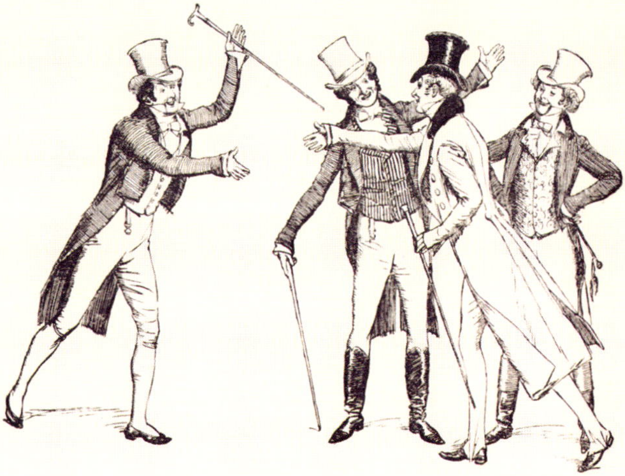

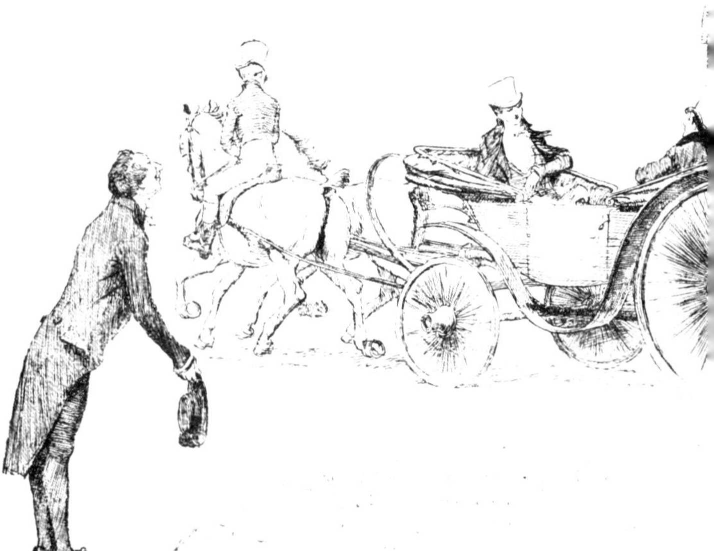

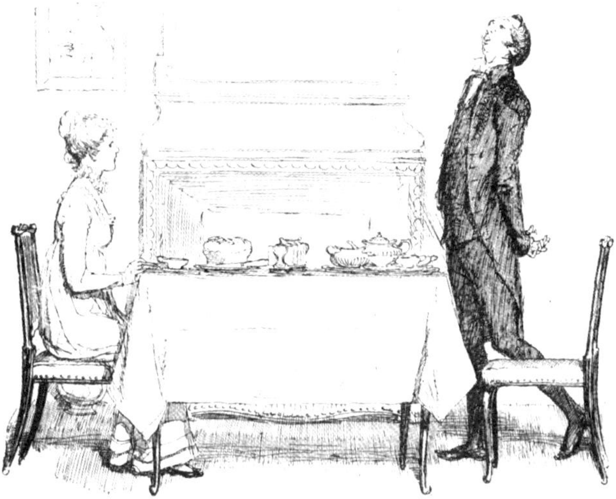

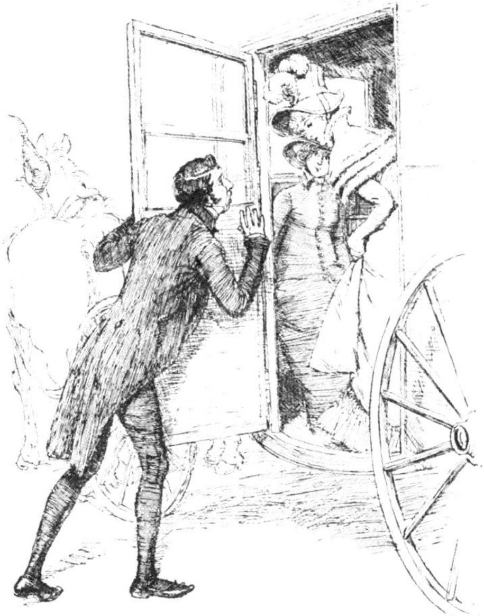

"我们这样挤在一起,有多带劲!"
"How nicely we are crammed in!"

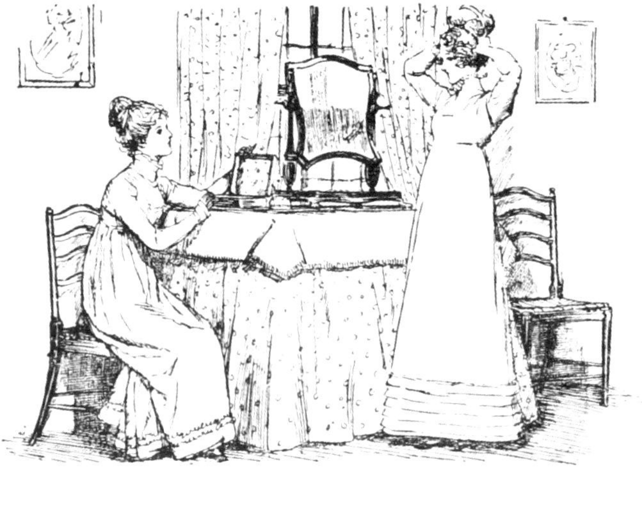

"我可下定了决心,再也不向任何人提起这件事。"

"For my part, I am determined never to speak of it again to anybody."

"当年米勒上校那一团人调走的时候……"
"...when Colonel Miller's regiment went away."

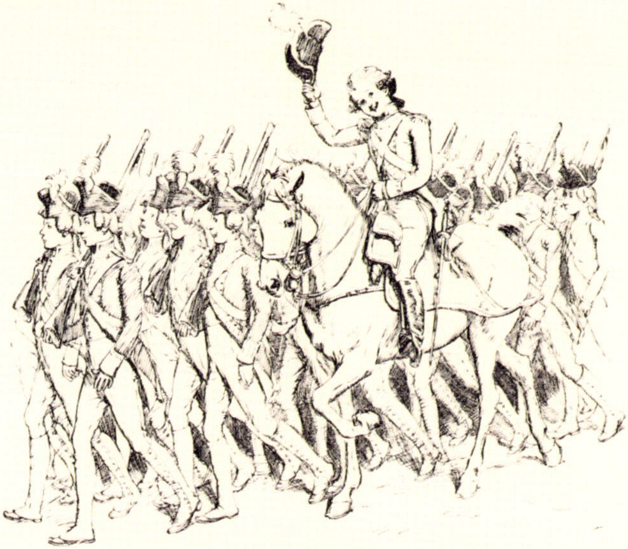

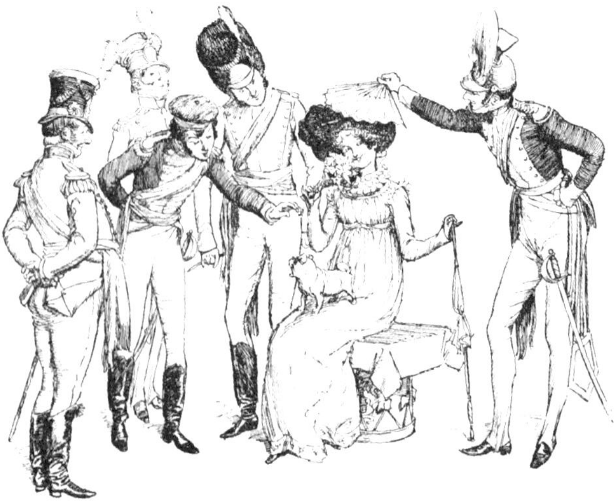

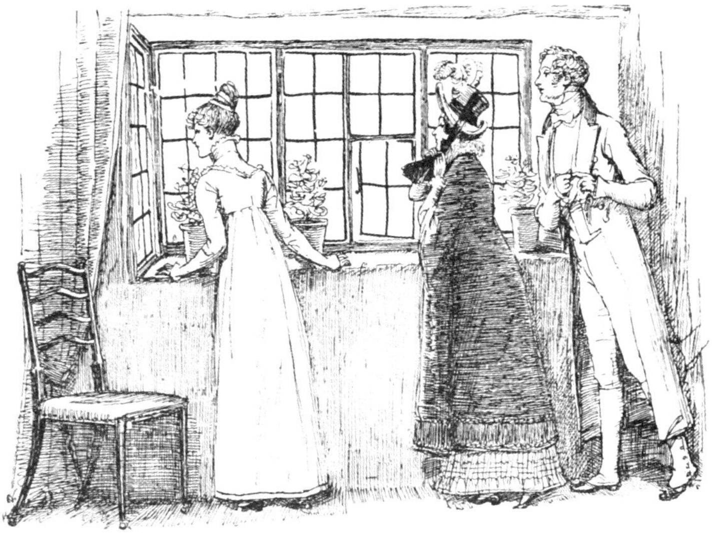

"You might have talked to me more when you came to dinner."
"A man who had felt less, might."

"假如不是那么爱你,或许倒可以多谈谈。"

"Howsoever that may be, you are grievously to be pitied, in which opinion I am not only joined by Mrs. Collins, but likewise by Lady Catherine and her daughter, to whom I have related the affair."

"曾以此事奉告。"

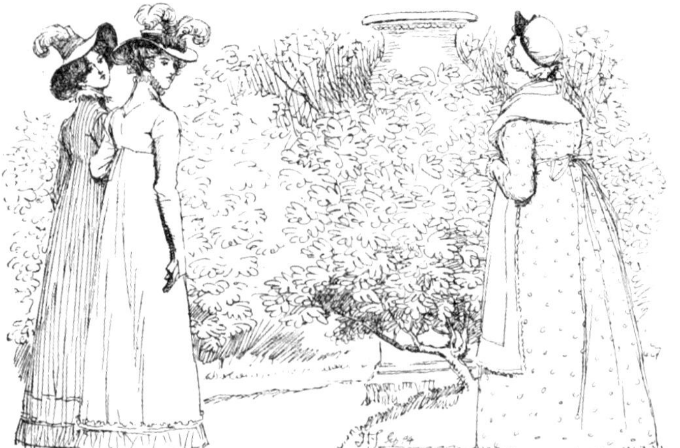

"也许你倒高兴看一看。"

...perhaps you would like to read it."

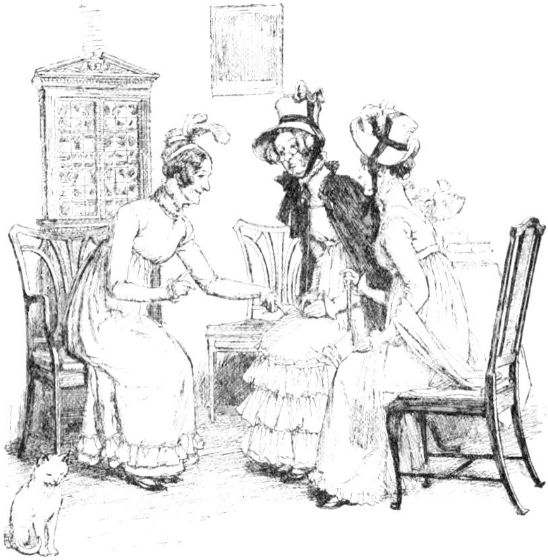

"If she heard me, it was by good luck, for I am sure she did not listen."

"我的话她听也不要听。"

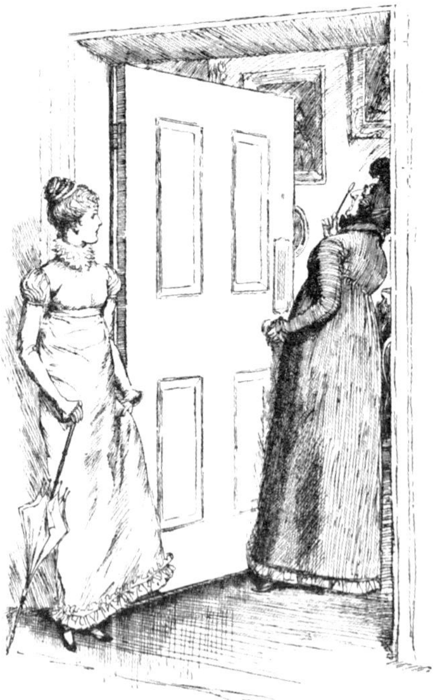

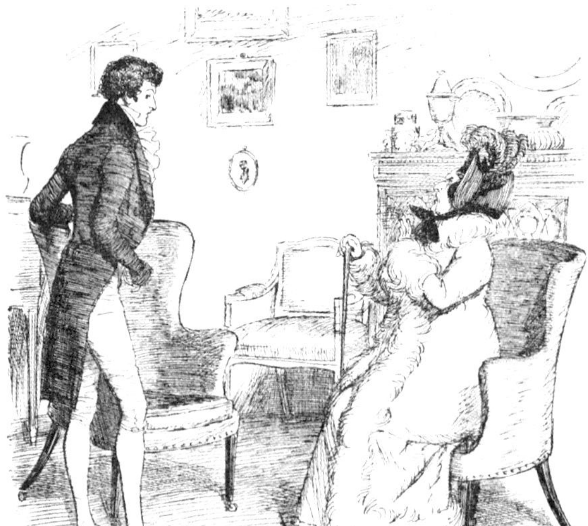

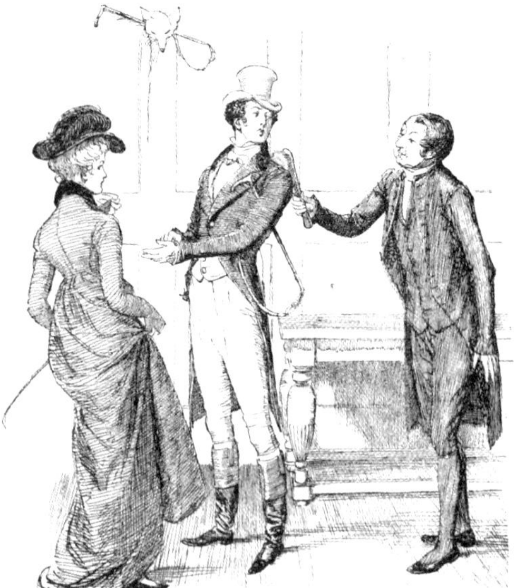

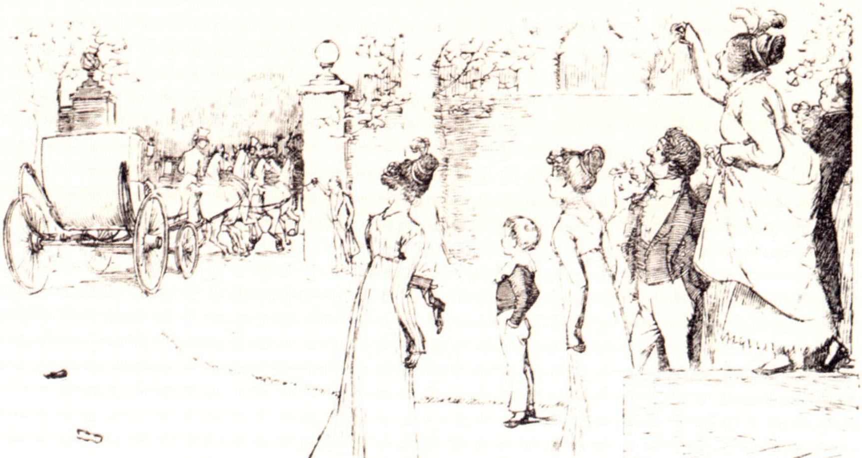

插图选自英国 George Allen 出版社 1894 年出版的《傲慢与偏见》（Pride and Prejudice）

图书在版编目（CIP）数据

《傲慢与偏见》艺术笔记/（英）简·奥斯丁著；
（英）休·汤姆森绘；孙致礼译. -- 北京：人民文学出版社，2017
ISBN 978-7-02-012853-2

Ⅰ.①傲…Ⅱ.①简…②休…③孙…Ⅲ.①长篇小说－英国－近代Ⅳ.①I561.44

中国版本图书馆CIP数据核字(2017)第109719号

责任编辑	朱卫净　尚　飞　张玉贞
装帧设计	陈　晔
出版发行	人民文学出版社
社　　址	北京市朝内大街166号
邮政编码	100705
网　　址	http://www.rw-cn.com
印　　刷	上海盛通时代印刷有限公司
经　　销	全国新华书店等
字　　数	7千字
开　　本	890毫米×1240毫米 1/32
印　　张	6
版　　次	2017年8月北京第1版
印　　次	2017年8月第1次印刷
书　　号	978-7-02-012853-2
定　　价	68.00元

如有印装质量问题，请与本社图书销售中心调换。电话：010-65233595